50 NIFTY PAPER CRAFTS

Written by Holly Hebert

Illustrated by Eve Guianan

Lowell House House
Juvenile
Los Angeles

CONTEMPORARY BOOKS
Chicago

NOTE

The numbered octopus in the upper right-hand corner of each craft indicates the level of difficulty; 1 being the easiest, 3 being the hardest.

Publisher: Jack Artenstein
Vice President, General Manager, Juvenile Publishing: Elizabeth Amos
Director of Publishing Services: Rena Copperman
Editorial Director: Brenda Pope-Ostrow
Senior Editor: Amy Downing
Art Director: Lisa-Theresa Lenthall
Typesetting and Layout: Michele Lanci-Altomare
Crafts Artist: Charlene Olexiewicz
Cover Photo: Ann Bogart

Lowell House books can be purchased at special discounts when ordered in bulk for premiums and special sales. Contact Department JH at the following address:

Lowell House Juvenile
2029 Century Park East, Suite 3290
Los Angeles, CA 90067

Library of Congress Catalog Card Number: 95-9490

ISBN: 1-56565-275-4

10 9 8 7 6 5 4 3 2 1

THE BAND OF FRIENDS

Make this cool chain bracelet with a friend. The wearer of the band promises to keep its secret, as well as your tight friendship.

WHAT YOU'LL NEED

- scissors ● ruler ● pen ● plain white paper ● clear tape
- light-colored tissue paper (not the waxy kind; use the softer gift-wrap kind)

DIRECTIONS

1 Cut a 3-inch-by-24-inch strip from the tissue paper. Now think about your special friend. What makes this person so unique? Does he or she tell funny stories, or help you out with homework? Use your pen to express how you feel about your friend on one side of the tissue. In your best handwriting, copy down what you've written on a separate sheet of paper and set it aside.

2 Fold the tissue into thirds lengthwise. Now take one end of the tissue in your fingers and begin twisting in one direction. Wet your fingers slightly to help get a tighter twist. The tissue should begin to look like a thick string. If you accidentally break the strand while twisting, don't panic. Just tape it back together and continue twisting.

3 When you've twisted the entire length of your tissue, tape the two ends and bring them together. Bring the top tissue string over and under the bottom string in a simple knot and pull both ends until the knot is a little smaller than a penny in the middle of your tissue string. Continue stacking loose knots until there is not enough tissue string to form another knot.

4 Use the remaining tissue string to tie the bracelet around your friend's wrist. Apply a very small piece of clear tape around the knot to secure it. Give him or her the copy of the words you wrote on the bracelet. Now only you and your friend know the secret message that makes this band a true tie!

UFO FRAME

Martians peek out from the corners of this funky frame—a perfect gift for one of your out-of-this-world friends!

WHAT YOU'LL NEED

- piece of thin, smooth cardboard, 6 inches by 14 inches
- scissors • masking tape • glue • photograph
- two large paper clips, each about 2 inches long
- four 4-inch squares of dual-colored paper (such as origami paper)
- sheet of green construction paper
- scraps of different-colored construction paper

DIRECTIONS

1 Fold the cardboard in half by bringing the two 6-inch edges of the sheet together. The half facing you will be the front of the frame. Cut a piece of masking tape about 4 inches long and set it aside. Cut another piece of masking tape about 2 inches long and tape it to the middle section of your 4-inch strip of tape, sticky sides together. The masking tape should now be sticky on both ends, but not in the middle. Hold the cardboard frame in an upside-down V shape. You will make the frame a triangular shape by securing one end of the tape strip to the center of one flap end to the bottom edge of the back side of the frame. Now your frame should stand on its own.

2 Glue your photo to the center of the front of the frame. Clip the two paper clips to the sides in the two top front corners. The paper clips should stick out about an inch from the frame.

3 Lay one of the 4-inch squares of dual-colored paper on a flat surface. Fold it in half on the diagonal, then unfold. Starting at one corner, making creases parallel to the center crease, make accordion pleats on the diagonal approximately ½ inch wide. An accordion pleat can be made by folding the bottom edge up ½ inch, flipping the paper over and around (so the fold on the bottom edge is now the top edge), and folding the top edge down ½ inch. You may have to cheat the folds slightly to include the center crease in your accordion pleats. Repeat the process until the entire length is folded.

4 Open the pleated paper at the center crease and flatten. The folded strip now shows colored squares. Repeat for all four pieces. Glue one folded strip to each of the four sides of your picture frame.

5 Out of the green construction paper cut four same-sized circles each about 1½ inches in diameter. These are your Martian heads. Dab glue on two of the circles and place one, glue side facing you, on the back of each paper clip. Now take the two remaining circles and place them on the front of each paper clip. Pinch the paper circles together and set aside to dry.

6 Use scissors to cut the colored construction paper scraps into eyes, ears, mouth, and—don't forget!—antennas for your Martian heads. Glue features in place. A picture of your friends will look great with these crazy creatures!

THE PAPER CONCORDE

This quick jet is your supersonic transport to high altitude. Okay, maybe it doesn't break sound barriers, but it's sure to outfly the competition!

WHAT YOU'LL NEED

- sheet of plain white paper, 8½ by 11 inches • paper clip • colored markers

DIRECTIONS

1 On a flat surface, fold your sheet of paper in half lengthwise and open it again. Fold the right bottom and top corners to the middle crease—the paper now forms a point at one end (see illustration). Fold paper in half again lengthwise (corners are on the inside) and lay it flat.

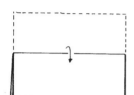 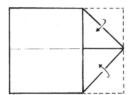 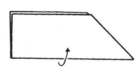

2 With the point in the lower right corner, take the entire top edge on the unfolded side and fold it down to meet the center fold. Flip paper over and do the same to the other side.

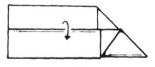

3 Now for the secret superspeed attachment—a paper clip applied to the pointed nose of your jet to make it twice as fast! Use colored pens to draw your name or personal logo across the top of the Paper Concorde's wings. When you are ready to take off, throw your craft at a slightly upward angle while calling out, "Blast off!"

FREDDY, THE JUMPING FROGLET

Freddy is a prince of a frog, but when you pet his back, he gets jumpy!

WHAT YOU'LL NEED

- 3-by-5-inch plain index card ● dark pen

DIRECTIONS

1 Lay the card on a flat surface in front of you, lengthwise. Take the upper right-hand corner and fold it across and down so the top edge lines up with the left-hand long edge. Take the upper left corner and fold it down, exactly over the triangle shape. Unfold the card and lay it flat lengthwise. At the point where the two creases that you just made cross, fold the upper section back, away from you. Make a sharp crease and unfold.

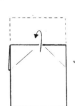

2 Now, along the one short straight line, pinch the two sides into each other. The card should fold in toward you, forming an arrow. Flatten the arrow.

3 Fold the outer corners of the arrow up to meet in the middle at the arrow's point. Fold both sides of your card so the edges meet each other in the middle.
Fold the bottom edge to meet the tip of your arrow, and make a crease.

  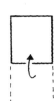

4 Now take this bottom edge (the flat side) and fold it down in half to the new bottom fold. Flip the card over. Your frog is in fine form! Use the dark pen to give Freddy eyes brimming with personality. He'll jump when you lightly stroke his back. If your friends make frogs, too, you can hold a frog-jumping contest!

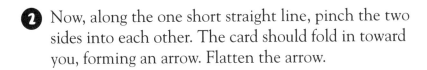

AFRICAN BEAUTY BEADS

Adult Supervision Recommended

Get artsy! Using the pages of an old magazine to create a festive bead necklace is recycling at its finest.

WHAT YOU'LL NEED

- magazine • ruler • dark pen • scissors
- toothpick • glue • needle • thread or thin yarn

DIRECTIONS

1 Tear four or five colorful pages from a magazine. On each page, measure and, with a ruler, draw straight lines the length of the magazine page $1\frac{1}{2}$ inches apart. Use your ruler to help you draw a diagonal line from the bottom left-hand corner of the page to the top point of the first line. Then draw a diagonal line from the top point of the first line to the bottom of the second line. Repeat, drawing diagonal lines between every lengthwise line.

2 Cut along the diagonal and vertical lines to make several triangular strips. Place a toothpick on the wide end of one strip. Begin rolling the strip tightly around the toothpick until the entire length is rolled. You should be able to see the different layers of magazine rolled around one another.

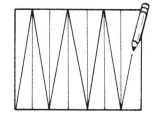

3 Smear glue with your fingertip under the corner flap of the rolled-up bead and over the entire bead to keep it intact. Remove the bead from the toothpick and set aside to dry. Continue making beads until you have enough to create the size necklace you want.

4 When your beads are dry, an adult can help you thread a needle, tying one end of the string or yarn off with a large knot. String your colorful beads through their hollow centers. When finished stringing, tie a sturdy knot with the ends of the string to complete the circle of your necklace. Make sure the necklace is wide enough to pull on and off over your head.

FISH OUT OF WATER

What fish is happier sitting on your dresser than swimming in a brook?
This sensational soft sculpture fish made from a simple lunch sack.

WHAT YOU'LL NEED

- old newspaper • paper lunch sack • large rubber band • scissors
- construction paper • glue • poster paint • paintbrushes

DIRECTIONS

1 Wad up pages of newspaper and stuff them into the lunch sack until it is half full. Pull the top of the sack together and cinch with the large rubber band at approximately the middle of the sack. Fan the top of the sack out and lay it down on the table. The fanned-out top will be the tail of the fish.

2 Cut out a large fin (called a dorsal fin) from the paper for the top of the fish's back. Cut out two smaller fins for the sides. Make a ½-inch fold along the bottom of the three fins. Glue these folds to the top and sides of the fish so your fish's fins will stick out a bit, away from its body. Let it dry.

3 Cover your work area with newspaper. Use poster paint to cover your fish with a bright tropical design, and give your fish two eyes and a cute set of lips. Cover the sides and top of your fish with paint and set the unpainted bottom of your fish on a piece of newspaper until the sides and top are dry.

4 When the paint is dry, paint your fish's belly. Let your fish dry on the newspaper again, this time setting it on its side. Remember, this fish makes a great pet as long as you don't get it wet!

SOFT HEART BRACELET

Everyone loves a softy! Show your heart to someone you care about with a sweet sculptured bracelet.

WHAT YOU'LL NEED

- thin cardboard, 1½ inches wide and 10 inches long • glue
- two paper clips • fourteen 6-inch pink tissue-paper squares
- fourteen 3-inch pink tissue-paper squares
- scissors • sheet of red tissue paper

DIRECTIONS

1 Form the cardboard strip into a circle, overlapping the two ends by 1½ inches. Apply glue to the overlapping section of the circle. Use two paper clips to secure the top and bottom of the overlapping ends. Set aside to dry.

2 Wad one 6-inch pink tissue square into a ball. Place the ball in the center of a 3-inch tissue square. Squeeze a thin line of glue around the edges of the smaller square. Gather the four corners together around the wad of tissue and twist. You now have a tissue-paper "stone" with a tail. Repeat until you have fourteen tissue-paper stones.

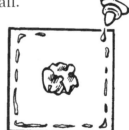 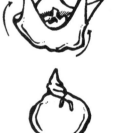

3 Cut the sheet of red tissue paper into a strip 7 inches wide by 12 inches long. Fold it in half lengthwise.

4 Make sure that your cardboard bracelet is dry, then remove the paper clips. Apply glue all around the outside of the bracelet. Place the bracelet in the center of one end of the folded strip of red tissue paper. There should be an equal amount of tissue on either side of the cardboard. Press the tissue onto the bracelet and roll the bracelet to the end of the tissue strip. The red tissue now covers the outside of your bracelet. Glue the end of the tissue to the bracelet to keep it in place.

5 Tuck the tissue that is sticking out from the sides of the cardboard through the bracelet's center and glue it around the inside of the bracelet.

6 Now take two of your pink tissue stones and twist their tails together, forming a heart. Repeat until you have seven hearts. Glue the tissue hearts to 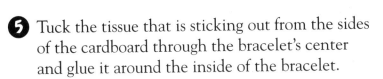 your bracelet, spacing them evenly around the outside. Once the glue has dried, give this bracelet to your favorite sweetheart of a friend!

FINGER FORTUNE-TELLER

Are you psychic? Your friends will think so when you play this fold-up wonder game. Telling fortunes was never so easy!

WHAT YOU'LL NEED

- a friend ● 8-inch square of plain white paper ● pen

DIRECTIONS

1 Fold the square in half. Fold it in half again to make a smaller square. Unfold the paper flat. The paper should appear to have four squares that join in the center.

2 Take each corner and fold it into the center. Turn over and fold the four new corners into the center. Again, turn the paper over.

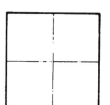

3 Fold the paper in half horizontally (so that the fold comes out toward you) and then unfold. Fold the paper in half vertically the same way, but leave folded.

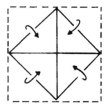 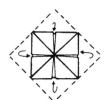

4 Slip each index finger under a pocket of the back fold and each thumb into a pocket of the front fold. Make sure your fingers are all the way up into the corners of these four separate pockets. Carefully bring all four corners together. The fortune-teller moves back and forth when you move your index fingers together and thumbs together. It moves side to side when you move your left finger and thumb together and your right finger and thumb together. Practice moving your fingers back and forth and sideways to operate the fortune-teller.

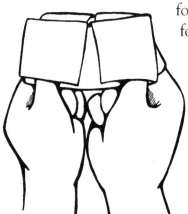

5 Take your fingers out of the fortune-teller and lay it flat on the table so the side with all four finger pockets faces you. Using a pen, number each pocket 1 through 4. Then turn the fortune-teller over and number the inside of each triangle 5 through 12. Open each of the four larger triangles and write a zany fortune on the inside.

Examples:
"Your allowance will be raised."
"You have a secret admirer."
"Your brainpower triples tonight."

6 Fold the triangles back in and you are ready to play.

7 Tell your friend to pick a number on the outside of the fortune-teller. Then open and close the fortune-teller that many times, moving your fingers side to side and back and forth. Have your friend pick a number on the inside of the fortune-teller. Again open and close it that many times, switching between side to side and back and forth. Have your friend pick a final number from the inside of the fortune-teller. The magic fortune-teller reveals all when you open the triangle flap bearing that number. In an eerie voice, speak the fortune!

YOU-DESIGN-IT PAPER DOLL

Create a fashion world of fresh possibilities for your own hip paper doll.

WHAT YOU'LL NEED

- glue • sheets of plain white paper • ruler • medium-thick cardboard
- pencil • colored pens • scissors

DIRECTIONS

1 Glue a piece of plain white paper to your cardboard piece and allow to dry. Draw the shape of your paper doll, at least 5 inches tall and 3 inches wide, on the paper-and-cardboard piece. When you have a shape you like, draw over the line you made with your pencil with a dark pen.

2 Now use your colored pens to draw the doll's facial features, hands, and feet inside the doll's outline. Then cut out your doll.

3 Make clothes for your paper doll by tracing around the whole doll onto a piece of white paper and then drawing in the item of clothing you'd like it to wear. If you have a whole outfit in mind, draw all the pieces on one sheet, such as a matching vest and jeans with a cool pair of clogs. Make a clear outline around each item of clothing.

4 Add tabs about ½ inch square around the clothing's outline. Add one to each shoulder and one to each side of tops. Add one to each hip and one on each side of skirts, pants, and shorts. For dresses, add tabs at each shoulder and each hip. Cut out the item of clothing, and cut off anything that isn't clothed or tabbed, such as the head and hands. Fold the tabs around the edges of your paper doll to keep the clothing in place.

RAINY-DAY HORSESHOES

A rainy day doesn't mean a boring day. It's a blast when you gather a few buddies to pitch horseshoes—indoor style!

WHAT YOU'LL NEED

- pencil • several pieces of thick cardboard • ruler • scissors • glue
- empty paper-towel roll • plain paper plate • masking tape

DIRECTIONS

1 With a pencil, draw a horseshoe shape on a piece of cardboard. The horseshoe is a U shape about 6 inches tall and 6 inches wide. The U shape should be about an inch thick. Cut it out, and continue tracing the horseshoe shape and cutting until you have eighteen horseshoes.

2 Each finished horseshoe will be made up of three cutouts. Apply glue to the first horseshoe. Lay a second horseshoe on top so they stack up evenly. Apply glue to the second horseshoe and lay the third on top. Set aside to dry. Repeat the steps to make six horseshoes. Glue the paper-towel roll standing upright to the center of the underside of the paper plate. Set aside to dry.

3 When all pieces are dry, cut a piece of duct tape and wrap it around the base of the paper-towel roll, reinforcing its connection to the paper plate. Set the paper plate (with the paper-towel roll standing straight up like a post) on the floor at one end of the room. If it's okay with an adult, cut another piece of duct tape and secure the plate to the floor so your post will not move.

4 Now you're ready to play! The object is to throw the horseshoe so that it lands around the post. Standing about 10 feet from the post, players alternate turns throwing three horseshoes per turn. Scoring is as follows: A ringer is 10 points; horseshoe touching post is 5 points; and horseshoe touching plate is 1 point. The player with the most points after the fifth turn is the winner!

RENAISSANCE HAT

This hat is historic high style! When you place it on your head, yesterday's news becomes tomorrow's fashion headlines.

WHAT YOU'LL NEED

• newspaper • clear tape • poster paint • paintbrush

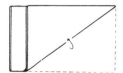

DIRECTIONS

1 Spread two equal-sized pieces of newspaper, one atop the other, on a flat surface, with the long edge right in front of you. Work with the two layers as if they were one, making all the folds with both sheets. Take the bottom right corner and fold it up diagonally toward the top left corner until the right corner aligns with the top edge. The corners will not completely match up. Take the long folded edge and turn it up into an additional fold about 2 inches high. This cuff will be the headband of the hat. Flip the paper over.

2 Take the bottom left corner of the triangle and fold it in toward the bottom right corner, stopping when the end is just over two-thirds of the way across. Now take the bottom right corner and fold it in toward the bottom left corner, stopping when the end meets the folded edge. Secure the overlapping cuffs together with clear tape, especially on the outside edge.

3 Fold the top of the triangle straight down and tuck it into the headband cuff of your hat. Tape down any edges that don't conform to the rounded structure of your hat. Line your work area with newspaper. Decorate your Renaissance hat with rich purple and deep blue poster paints. Let your hat dry in an upright position (as if it were on your head).

FANS OF FANS

Make a hot-weather helper that is cool enough to beat the heat!

WHAT YOU'LL NEED

● butcher paper ● colored pens ● scissors ● yarn ● two thumbtacks (optional)

DIRECTIONS

1 Draw a circle approximately 2 feet in diameter on the butcher paper. (Tracing the bottom of a round garbage container is an easy way to make an accurate circle.) Fold the circle in half, and cut out the semicircle.

2 Use your pens to decorate the entire shape with any design you like, leaving as little white space as possible. Large flowers, wavy stripes, or a colorful map of the world make mighty fine designs!

3 Make accordion pleats about an inch wide from bottom to top. An accordion pleat can be made by folding the bottom edge up an inch, flipping the paper over and around (so the front of the bottom edge is now the back of the top edge), and folding the top edge down an inch. Repeat the process until the entire length is folded.

4 Gather together the accordion pleats along the folded edge, or bottom, of your fan and wrap it tightly with yarn. Wind yarn around the base of the fan until the handle is secure. Yarn should wind up the base about 3 inches from the bottom of the fan. Tie the yarn and trim off any extra yarn.

5 Pull the accordion pleats open to "fan out" your fan. When you are not using your fan to cool off, use it just to *look* cool by tacking it up as a wall decoration! Use two thumbtacks (for the left and right edges of the fan) to display your creation.

CLUB MEMBERS' BEST VESTS

Gather friends together to express your collective creativity. Matching club vests will show the world your group spirit. All for one and one for all!

WHAT YOU'LL NEED

- standard-size brown paper grocery bag • scissors • clear tape
- newspaper • poster paint in two or three colors • paintbrushes • glue

DIRECTIONS

1 To make one vest, flatten a grocery bag out on an even surface with the open end toward you. Cut directly up the center of the front of the grocery bag. Be sure not to cut the back of the bag!

2 Connected to the center cut you just made, cut a hole out of the bag's bottom that you could fit your neck through. Approximate where your arms would be on the sides of the vest and cut a circle about 5 inches in diameter out of each side of the bag for armholes. You now have the beginnings of a fabulous vest.

3 Try your vest on for size (open side in front). Your friends can help you make any adjustments needed, such as larger neck- or armholes. Make your vest more comfortable by taping down any folds or rough edges that might occur around the neck- or armholes. To give your vest a lapel, fold the top corners on either side of the front opening down and away about 3 inches.

4 Cover your work area with newspaper. If your vest has a store's name on the outside, carefully turn your vest inside out. Decorate the front of your vest with painted stripes, polka dots, or the name of your club. Set aside to dry. When the front is dry, turn your vest over and print your name across the top of the back side. Allow paint to dry, then your vest is ready to wear—and match with your pals!

STAR STATIONERY

This star design turns plain paper into letter heaven!

WHAT YOU'LL NEED

- pen or pencil • several sheets of plain, light-colored paper • scissors
- 4-inch square of thick cardboard • newspaper • different colors of poster paint • small tins or plastic dishes, one per paint color
- thin paintbrushes, less than $1/2$ inch wide

DIRECTIONS

1 Copy the star pattern shown here onto a piece of plain white paper. Carefully cut out the star and place it on one side of the thick cardboard square. Trace the cutout directly onto the cardboard square a few times and cut out the cardboard stars. These stars will be your stamps.

2 Cover your work area with newspaper. Pour a different color of poster paint into each tin or plastic dish.

3 With a paintbrush, paint a cardboard star with a single coat of paint, then press it around the border of a fresh, plain sheet of paper. Take another star, paint it with another color, and press it in a different spot along the edge of the paper. Continue to decorate your sheets of paper with different-colored stars. (Be sure to leave room on your stationery to write!) When your stationery is dry, write a colorful note to someone special, telling them why you think they're a star, too!

ONE STEP FURTHER

Once you get the hang of this, you may want to try your own design. How about a wild animal or cool tropical scenery? Just use a pencil to draw the image on a new cardboard square, cut it out, dip it in paint, and create your own personalized stationery.

I-GOT-RHYTHM STICK

Keep the beat or set your own, with a rhythm-stick shaker that gets you moving!

WHAT YOU'LL NEED

- masking tape • empty toilet-paper roll • ¼ cup dried lentils or beans
- pencil • construction paper in different colors • scissors
- ruler • white glue

DIRECTIONS

1 Use masking tape to seal off one end of an empty toilet-paper roll. Pour ⅓ cup of dried lentils or beans inside the sealed-off toilet-paper roll. Seal the open end of the toilet-paper roll with masking tape. Shake the instrument to make sure there are no open spaces for the lentils or beans to spill out. Some beans will stick to the masking tape inside the roll—this is okay.

2 Trace the circular end of your shaker onto construction paper two times. Cut out the two circles and set aside. Cut a strip 5 inches wide and 6 inches long from any color of construction paper.

3 Cut shapes such as little circles, triangles, or squiggles out of different-colored pieces of construction paper. Use the glue to attach the cutout shapes to one side of the construction-paper strip. Allow to dry.

4 Spread glue around the outside of your shaker. Cover the shaker with the construction-paper strip, decorated side out. Trim the paper so it is flush with the ends of the toilet-paper tube. Glue one construction-paper circle to each end of the shaker. Set aside to dry.

5 Practice moving your shaker in time to a song on the radio or your favorite tape. Many professional musicians use instruments similar to your rhythm shaker to keep the beat!

SIDE-BY-SIDE FRIENDS STREAMER

United they stand. . . . A long streamer of side-by-side wacky friends cheers up any room. For maximum effect, hang this streamer across a doorway, or use it to decorate the trim of your bedroom wall.

WHAT YOU'LL NEED

- sheet of butcher paper, 3 feet in length • scissors • pencil • clear tape
- paper hole punch • scraps of colored paper • glue

DIRECTIONS

1 Lay out your sheet of butcher paper and fold in half lengthwise. Fold in half lengthwise again. Open the sheet flat. Cut along the folded creases so that you have four long strips of butcher paper.

2 Take one of the butcher-paper strips and fold it in half, short ends together. Continue to fold it in half until your folded piece is approximately the size you'd like each cutout friend in the chain to be.

3 With your pencil, draw an outline of a person on the top of your folded butcher-paper strip. The friend's arms and legs should reach to the very side edges of the paper. When you like the shape of your outline, cut out the doll, cutting through *all* the layers of paper. Note: Arms and legs are not cut out where they meet the end of the paper. Now open your chain of friends!

4 To make your chain longer, repeat Steps 2 and 3 using the other three strips of butcher paper. Connect the streamers to each other with clear tape.

5 Use the paper hole punch on colored construction paper to make small cutout circles for eyes, cheeks, and mouths. Decorate each friend in the chain and give each its own wacky personality!

 # THE FUNNIEST JOKE BOOK EVER

Heard any good jokes lately? Keep a record of the most hilarious ones by writing them down in this book made especially for laughs.

WHAT YOU'LL NEED

- blank 8½-by-11-inch sheet of paper • scissors • pen
- crayons or colored pencils

DIRECTIONS

1 Fold one sheet of paper in half lengthwise. Fold in half again, short ends together. Fold in half one last time, short ends together. Open the paper fully. It is now divided into eight equal parts.

2 Fold paper in half widthwise. Cut from the center of the folded edge straight along the crease to the middle of the page where the four folds meet.

3 Open the paper fully. Fold paper in half lengthwise. Grab one short end with your left hand and one with your right. Push the left and right ends toward each other to meet in the center. Fold the pages around to form a book. The book has a front and back cover and six pages.

4 Using your crayons or colored pencils and pen, design the cover of your joke book. A cool design could include stripes, polka dots, or huge flowers. Now every time you hear a joke you'd like to retell, jot it down on the pages of this book. Don't forget to name this book with a clever title!

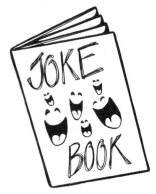

COOL COLLAGE BOOK COVER

Personalize and protect your favorite book with a dazzling collage of activities, people, and images.

WHAT YOU'LL NEED

- standard-size brown paper grocery bag • scissors • hardback book
- pencil • magazine • glue

DIRECTIONS

1 Cut up any folded crease across the length of a brown paper bag to the bottom. Cut off just the bottom of the bag. Lay the bag out flat, then open the book you want to cover and place it spine-side down on the paper bag, somewhere near the center. Draw a line on the bag with the pencil along the top and bottom of your book. Remove the book. Turn the top and bottom edges of the bag in by folding along the pencil lines you just drew.

2 Once again place your book open in the center of the folded bag. Now the top and bottom of the book should be flush with the folded edges of the paper bag. Slip the left side of the bag over the book's hard front cover. Then feed the back cover of the book inside the folds of the other side of your paper book cover. Close the newly covered book to make sure the cover fits snugly.

3 Cut out pictures of your favorite activities or celebrities, interesting words from headlines, or even just colors you like from a magazine. Arrange the cutouts on your book cover. When you're pleased with the arrangement, use a small amount of glue to attach each picture to your book cover. Now your book is not only protected from wear and tear, it shows off your personal style, too!

SEEING SPOTS!

Adult Supervision Required

Dots galore in spectacular shapes and crazy colors change this plain tissue paper into an optical wonder. It can be a cool wall hanging, dresser cover, or a very special piece of wrapping paper.

WHAT YOU'LL NEED

- white tissue paper (soft, not shiny) ● paper towels ● plain scratch paper
- mixing bowl filled with water ● felt-tipped pens (water soluble)
- iron ● ironing board

DIRECTIONS

1 Take the shorter sides of the tissue paper and begin folding the paper into accordion pleats about 3 inches wide until you have one vertical strip of folded paper. An accordion pleat is made by folding the bottom edge of your paper up 3 inches, flipping the paper over and around (so the front of the bottom edge is now the top edge), and folding the top edge down 3 inches. Repeat the process until the entire length is folded.

2 Place the strip in front of you horizontally. Take the left one-third and fold it over the strip. Then take the right one-third and fold it under the strip. It should now be a small rectangle shape.

3 Lay paper towels over a piece of plain scratch paper. Place the folded tissue in a bowl of water until it is damp all the way through (about 10 seconds). Carefully take the tissue out of the water and place it on the paper towels. Blot dry with additional paper towels.

4 Use a felt-tipped pen to draw dots and small circles on the damp folded-up tissue. Make circles by dotting your pen instead of pulling the pen along the delicate paper. Hold the pen in one position, letting the ink soak all the way through every layer of tissue, then move the pen to the next spot.

5 Press your damp rectangle shape with another piece of plain scratch paper for about 20 seconds. This distributes the ink more evenly through every tissue layer. Very carefully unfold your tissue and let it dry on a fresh layer of paper towels.

6 When the tissue paper has dried, ask an adult to iron it with a cool iron. This gives your paper a smooth finish. Now you're ready to hang it on the wall above your bed, or else wrap a special gift in it!

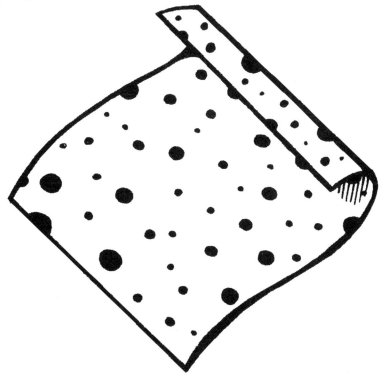

DRESSING UP THE SNEAKERS

This bow tie, which is traditionally worn with a button-down shirt, can add new pizzazz to—of all things—your tennis shoes!

WHAT YOU'LL NEED

- patterned gift wrap • scissors • two safety pins, approximately 1 inch long
- clear tape • two buttons, ½ inch to 1 inch wide • strong craft glue

DIRECTIONS

1 Cut a 4-inch square out of the gift wrap. Fold the square into accordion pleats about ½ inch wide. An accordion pleat is made by folding the bottom edge up ½ inch, flipping the paper over and around (so the front side of the bottom edge is now the back side of the top edge), and folding the top edge down ½ inch. Fan the bow tie at both ends, while you keep the center folded.

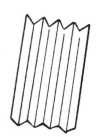

2 Cut a strip ¾ inch wide by 6 inches long out of the gift wrap. Wind strip around the center of the bow tie four times. Place an open safety pin against the paper strip, pointed pin out. Carefully wrap the remaining length of the paper strip around both the bow tie and the base of the safety pin, securing the pin to the bow tie. Tape the end of the strip down with clear tape.

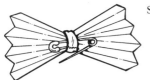

3 Position the safety pin so it is on the back side of your bow tie. On the front side of your bow tie, glue the button directly to the center of your paper strip. Allow to dry.

4 Repeat Steps 1 through 3 and make a second bow tie.

5 Pin your smart bow ties to each lace of a pair of tennis shoes—and you'll have the best-looking shoes on the block!

HANDFUL OF MONSTERS

Put on a crazy puppet show for your pals and family with these goofy creature finger puppets. Having a handful of monsters is particularly handy when it's your turn to entertain siblings or friends who are younger than you!

WHAT YOU'LL NEED

- colored construction paper • scissors • pencil
- multicolored scraps of paper • glue • thin black marker • clear tape

DIRECTIONS

1 Cut a 3-inch square out of the colored paper. Fold down the top edge of the square about ½ inch. Roll paper into a tube that is the size of your middle finger. Lightly pencil in the face of your puppet.

2 Unroll the tube and lay it flat. Cut out bits of the colored scrap paper and glue them to your puppet's face to create eyes, mouth, hair, eyebrows, ears, whiskers—all the crazy features you want your monster to have! Use a marker to add details to the puppet's scary face. Set aside to dry.

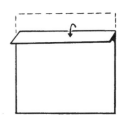

3 Once the glue has dried on your puppet, roll up the puppet again and size it to your finger, this time securing it with a piece of clear tape.

4 Make ten puppets for ten fingers. A full cast of characters can act out a spectacular monster mash matinee!

POP-UP BIRTHDAY CARD

Surprise a friend by making a personalized pop-up card.

WHAT YOU'LL NEED

- two pieces of light-colored construction paper, 8½ by 11 inches
- ruler • scissors • colored markers • pencil • paste or glue

DIRECTIONS

1 Fold one piece of construction paper in half widthwise to form a blank card. From the upper right-hand corner of the folded card, measure and cut out a square 3 inches in dimension.

2 Fold the left side of the card diagonally to the right edge of the card. Unfold. Open the card. Pinch the center crease of the middle portion of the card as you close the card, folding the center piece inside the card at an angle. Now the middle piece pops up when the card is opened.

3 With your scissors, round the edges of the pop-up piece, creating the top of an oval. Now use your colored markers to draw the bottom half of the oval. Inside the oval, draw a wacky, smiling face. Write a birthday salutation under the pop-up face, such as "Hope your birthday is wild fun—like you!"

4 Now fold the second piece of construction paper in half widthwise. Measure 3 inches down from the top of the card and mark it a few times. Cut off the top of the card along the small marks. This will be the outside of your card.

5 On the front of the outside card, decorate it and write "Happy Birthday!" in large letters. When you are happy with the way it looks, apply glue sparingly to its inside and set the pop-up section of your card within it (perfectly aligning the middle creases). Allow to dry.

SNAPPING LIZARD

A snapping desert lizard can be fierce or friendly—you decide!

WHAT YOU'LL NEED

- 8-inch square of dual-colored origami paper • black pen

DIRECTIONS

1 Fold the 8-inch square in half diagonally. Unfold. Place it in front of you in a diamond shape, crease running vertically. Take the left bottom edge and fold it flush with the center crease. Do the same with the right bottom edge.

2 Make sure the top point of the diamond is the wider point. Take the left top edge and fold it flush with the center crease. Do the same with the right top edge. Fold the bottom point up to the top point.

3 Take the right bottom corner and fold it flush with the center crease. Unfold. Take the left bottom corner and fold it flush with the center crease. Unfold. Open the bottom left corner of the triangle slightly and pinch the left crease of the triangle into the triangle's center. Do the same with the right lower corner. Flatten the top layer.

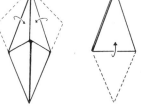

4 Fold the right half of the top layer of the diamond on top of the left half. Turn the form over and fold the bottom right layer on top of the bottom left layer. Pinch the bottom point of the diamond between your thumb and index finger. *Ta da!* You are making the lizard snap!

5 With your pen, draw teeth and eyes on the lizard. Remember, his snapping jaws can talk . . . or bite!

29

TOPSY TURTLE

This adorable soft sculpture turtle fits in the palm of your hand!

WHAT YOU'LL NEED

- cardboard egg carton • scissors • tissue paper in two different shades of green
- ruler • glue • black construction paper

DIRECTIONS

1 Cut out one section of a cardboard egg carton. Include part of the divider between eggs in your cutout section. That will be where Topsy's head goes.

2 Cut tissue paper into fourteen 6-inch squares (seven in each shade of green) and fourteen 3-inch squares (seven in each shade of green).

3 Wad one 6-inch square into a ball. Place the wadded piece in the center of a 3-inch square and dot glue along the edges of the 3-inch square. Gather the tissue square's edges and twist to make a tissue-paper "stone." Snip the tail off of your tissue ball and glue the tissue ball on the tail end of the Topsy structure. Repeat until Topsy is completely covered with green tissue stones.

4 Cut one 12-inch square of green tissue. Wad this square up and place it inside a 6-inch tissue square, making a tissue stone twice the size of the others. This big stone is Topsy's head. Glue it to the piece of egg carton divider on the Topsy structure. Set aside to dry.

5 Now cut eyes, a mouth, a small triangular tail, and four little feet from the black construction paper. Glue the features on Topsy. Allow to dry. Stick your new pet in your shirt pocket and pal around with it all day.

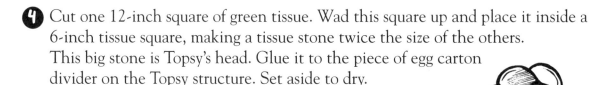

ACT IT OUT

Sharpen your acting skills and challenge your wits when you get together with friends for this imagination twister!

WHAT YOU'LL NEED

- at least three friends • empty facial-tissue box • two sheets of plain white tissue paper • pens or pencils • clear tape • scissors • colored felt-tipped markers • eight sheets of standard white paper, 8½ inches by 11 inches

DIRECTIONS

1 Wrap an empty facial-tissue box in two overlapping sheets of tissue paper as if you were wrapping a gift. Tape up the ends so the box is completely covered. Cut a hole in the tissue paper where the hole of the box is. Carefully tape the tissue paper around the hole to keep it from ripping. Use markers to decorate the tissue paper. On one side of the box, write ACTOR'S TOOLBOX.

2 Stack eight sheets of white paper on top of one another. Fold in half lengthwise, then widthwise. Unfold and cut along the creases. Split up the paper pieces equally among you and each friend. Tell your buddies to write on each of their strips the name of a living thing and a location. Then the players should fold up their strips and put them into the Actor's Toolbox.

3 One person picks a piece of paper out of the Actor's Toolbox. Without showing it to anyone else, the person acts out the character in the location—without saying a word! Other players try to guess the correct character and location. (Players can not guess at the strips they wrote.) The player who guesses correctly keeps the strip of paper with those answers on it. It is now that player's turn to pick a piece of paper from the Actor's Toolbox and act it out. At the end of the game, whoever has the most slips of paper wins!

26

FIREWORKS BOW

Packages burst with color when you crown them with this bright bow!

WHAT YOU'LL NEED

- red, orange, and yellow ribbon, about 1 inch wide • scissors
- ruler • glue • pencil

DIRECTIONS

1 Cut red and orange ribbon into foot-long strips, three in each color. Take one strip and glue the two ends together, slightly overlapping them to form a circle. Repeat for all strips.

2 Make each ribbon circle into a bow shape by pinching the top and bottom of the circle together. Dot glue on the insides of the ribbon where your fingers are holding the circle together. Your ribbon should look like a figure eight.

3 Crisscross two red bows to form an X. Glue them together in the center of the X. Add a third red bow across the center of the X and glue. Now add each orange bow at a diagonal atop the red bows, gluing each one in place at the center of the X.

4 Cut two 6-inch-long strips of yellow ribbon. Use the scissors to fray both ends of one yellow ribbon into several tiny strips, each less than $1/4$ inch wide and about $2\,1/2$ inches long. Curl each little cut strip of ribbon one at a time around a pencil, creating a spiral effect. Glue the uncut center inch of the strip to the center of your bow.

5 Glue together the ends of the remaining 6-inch yellow ribbon into a small circle, then glue the circle to the center of your bow. Glue your dynamite bow to the top of a special gift, and watch your friends "explode" with admiration!

A GULPING BIG VASE

Create a container for your favorite flowers in a vase designed by you!

WHAT YOU'LL NEED

- five sheets of tissue paper in several different colors ● scissors
- clean, dry, large-size paper cup (32-ounce cup works best) ● glue

DIRECTIONS

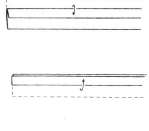

1 Cut different colors of tissue paper into long strips about 3 inches wide and 2 feet long. Fold the strip into thirds lengthwise. Start at one end of the tissue and begin twisting. Twist in one direction only. Wet your fingers slightly to help you get a tighter twist. The tissue will look like a thick string when you're finished. Make several long tissue strings in your favorite colors.

2 Apply glue around the outside of the cup, near the bottom. Wrap your paper string around the cup, pressing it into the glue as you go. Continue to spread the glue higher on the cup as you keep wrapping. Alternate colors and experiment with new patterns as you work your way up the cup. When you get to the top, your vase will be completely covered in your own design. Set aside to dry.

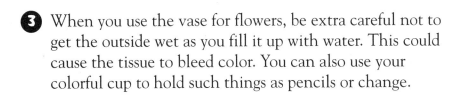

3 When you use the vase for flowers, be extra careful not to get the outside wet as you fill it up with water. This could cause the tissue to bleed color. You can also use your colorful cup to hold such things as pencils or change.

KOOKY CARTON TOTE

Adult Supervision Recommended

Craft a tote just the right size for on-the-go essentials such as paper, a pen, a brush, and even a mirror. Who would guess the bag you're cartin' is really a milk carton?

WHAT YOU'LL NEED

- colored tissue paper ● glue
- strip of thin cardboard, 1½ inches wide by 2½ feet long
- scissors ● ruler ● ½ gallon paper milk carton, washed and dried
- two metal paper fasteners ● clear tape

DIRECTIONS

1 Glue a layer of tissue paper evenly around the cardboard strip. Allow to dry. With an adult's help, take a pair of scissors and poke a hole in the center of the cardboard strip an inch from the right end. Poke another hole an inch from the left end.

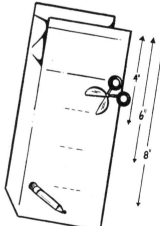

2 Unfold the top of the milk carton. On one side of the milk carton, measure 4 inches from the top. At this spot, have an adult help you make a horizontal cut 1½ inches wide in the center. Now measure 6 inches from the top and make another 1½-inch-wide horizontal cut parallel to the first one. Measure 8 inches from the top of the carton and make one more parallel cut 1½ inches wide.

3 Make the same three cuts on the opposite side of the milk carton. Then poke a hole with your scissors in the center, 1 inch from the bottom of the carton, on both sides with the parallel slits.

4 Feed one end of the cardboard strip into the top cut on one side from the outside of the carton. Then feed it back out through the second cut on the same side. Thread the cardboard strip back into the carton on the third cut. Push the end of the strip all the way down to the bottom of the carton. Poke a paper fastener through the holes at the bottom of the carton and the cardboard strip on the inside. Open the paper fastener flush with the inside of the milk carton.

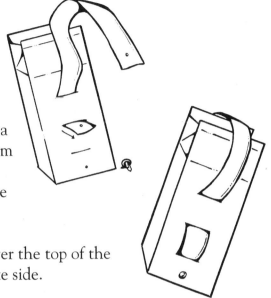

5 Bring the other end of the cardboard strip over the top of the milk carton and repeat Step 4 on the opposite side.

6 Spread glue around the outside of the carton. Roll the carton in a layer of tissue paper that sticks out approximately 4 inches from the bottom of the carton and at least 1 inch from the top. Glue the side tissue seam closed. Use the tissue overhang on the bottom of the carton to cover the bottom as if you were wrapping a gift, gluing tissue down. Neatly tape the overlapping top tissue inside the mouth of the carton.

7 You can decorate the outside of your tote by gluing tissue-paper strings and stones in various patterns. (See page 30 to learn how to make stones and page 33 to learn how to make strings.) Your crazy tote is now ready to be toted!

 # FANCY SHMANCY PAPER PLACE MAT

It's true, paper can be woven just like cloth! You'll love the look of this neatly textured place mat so much, you'll want to create a whole set!

WHAT YOU'LL NEED

- two 12-by-18-inch sheets of construction paper in different colors
- ruler • pencil • scissors • clear Con-Tact paper

DIRECTIONS

1 Lay one piece of construction paper in front of you so it is wider than it is tall. Use a ruler to measure and, with a pencil, draw a straight vertical line 1 inch in from the left edge. Do the same for the right edge.

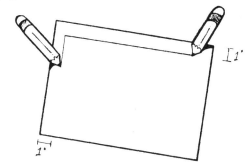

2 Now measure and draw a horizontal line 1 inch from the top of the construction paper within the borders on the left and right sides of the page. Measure 1 inch down from that line and draw another horizontal line within the left and right borders of the page. Continue drawing horizontal lines an inch apart until you reach the bottom of the page.

3 Cut along these horizontal lines, leaving an uncut 1-inch border around the four edges of the page.

4 On a second piece of construction paper, along the longer side, measure and draw vertical lines 1 inch apart. Cut along the lines from end to end, making long 1-inch strips.

5 Starting from the top left corner of the slitted construction paper, feed one construction-paper strip vertically through the horizontal slits in the following manner: over the first strip, under the second strip, over the third strip, under

the fourth strip, and so on. This process is called weaving. One at a time, weave each strip next to the previous strip through the slitted construction-paper sheet. Start your first strip in an over-under pattern, then weave the next strip in an under-over pattern. Each strip should have the opposite weaving pattern from the ones next to it. Continue weaving until you run out of room in your slitted construction paper. Trim the ends of the strips so they align neatly.

6 Erase any visible pencil marks. Carefully place the sticky side of a sheet of clear Con-Tact paper on top of your finished mat, then flip it over and place a piece of Con-Tact paper on the bottom of your mat, too. To keep Con-Tact paper from bubbling, it is helpful to apply it slowly, inch by inch, and have a friend help you smooth it onto the place mat as you go. Trim the edges.

ONE STEP FURTHER

These place mats make great gifts for grandparents and other relatives. Hand-deliver them in sets of four.

PSYCHEDELIC BUTTERFLY

When this butterfly hangs out near an open window, its psychedelic wings catch the cool breeze.

WHAT YOU'LL NEED

- dual-colored paper (such as gift wrap in a solid color), 12 inches wide by 20 inches long • scissors • ruler • clear tape • empty toilet-paper tube • solid colored paper • glue • dark pen • string

DIRECTIONS

1 Cut dual-colored paper into twenty 1-inch-wide, 1-foot-long strips.

2 Form a strip into a circle, the most colorful side facing out, and tape the edges together at a slight overlap with clear tape. Take another strip and form a slightly smaller circle that fits inside the first circle with slightly less than $1/2$ inch of space between the two circles all the way around. Tape this strip with clear tape and cut off the excess overlapping paper.

3 Continue making smaller circles until you have five circles nested inside one another. Pinch together the inside of the center circle and the outside of the largest circle so that all the circles are joined between your fingers. Secure tape at the point your fingers are joining the stack of circles. This is one of your butterfly's large top wings.

4 Repeat Steps 2 and 3 three times for the other top wing and two bottom wings. The bottom wings are slightly smaller in diameter than the top wings, so begin with a strip 10 inches long and leave less room between each circle.

5 Wrap an empty toilet-paper tube in a solid-colored paper. Glue seam where paper overlaps itself. Trim the paper flush to the ends of the toilet-paper tube. This will be the butterfly's body.

6 Glue each of the four wings one at a time to your butterfly's body, the larger wings first, then the smaller wings directly underneath the bigger ones. Hold the wing in place while the glue sets before moving to the next wing. Set aside to allow the glue to dry.

7 Use the pen to give your butterfly eyes on the upper part of its body. Cut two thin strips of paper and glue them to the butterfly's head for antennas. Put one end of a piece of string through the top of the butterfly's tube body. Bring string through the tube and back around the outside of it, tying the string to itself. Now your butterfly is ready to hang near a breezy window.

WINDOW OF WISHES

You don't have to wait until nightfall to wish on this tissue-paper window star!

WHAT YOU'LL NEED

- pencil ● two sheets of construction paper, 12 inches by 18 inches ● scissors ● glue ● different colors of tissue paper cut into ten strips, 2 inches wide and 18 inches long

DIRECTIONS

1 In a construction paper's center, draw the outline of a star about 3 inches wide. Outline the star by following the original line with your pencil about ¾ inch outside the first line. Continue drawing star outlines ¾ inch larger than the one before, leaving a 1-inch-wide border around the page.

2 Place the star sheet atop the blank piece of construction paper. Poke tip of scissors through both sheets of paper, then cut the star in the middle completely out. (Make sure to keep both pieces aligned with your free hand so you are cutting both pages exactly alike.) In the same way, cut along the line of the next-size star, but stop cutting when you get ½ inch from where you started the cut. Cut all of your outlines in the same fashion.

3 Go back and snip out every *other* star outline, cutting out the last ½ inch. Separate the two large pieces of construction paper. Lay tissue in different-colored stripes across the length of one piece of construction paper, securing them with glue along the 1-inch border. Apply glue around the edges of the second sheet of construction paper. Lining up the design with that of the first construction-paper piece, glue this second sheet to the layer of tissue paper. On both pieces of construction paper, glue the remaining star outlines to the tissue. Set aside to dry.

4 Now this picture-perfect work of art is ready to be hung in any window, looking as beautiful inside the house as outside.

QUICKIE MOUSE

Adult Supervision Recommended

This sassy little pet mouse can be put together in literally two minutes.
He's a loyal squeak whose favorite place to sit is on your shoulder.

WHAT YOU'LL NEED

- 3-inch square of colored paper • glue • scissors
- scraps of pink construction paper • pencil • pen • safety pin

DIRECTIONS

1 Fold paper square on the diagonal. Unfold. Hold in a diamond shape, with the crease pointing toward you. Fold the bottom left edge flush with the diagonal crease. Fold the bottom right edge flush with the diagonal crease. Fold the diagonal crease closed again, flaps inside. Let diagonal crease relax open so the fold is at a 45-degree angle. Pull one flap down and allow the other flap to follow. Glue overlapping flaps together. Set aside to dry. This is the body of your Quickie Mouse!

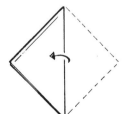   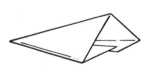

2 Cut circles for ears and a long strip for the tail from the pink paper. Roll the tail strip around a pencil to give it a corkscrew curl. Attach the ears and tail to your mouse with glue. Draw two tiny mouse eyes with a pen.

3 Have an adult help you poke the safety pin through the two overlapping bottom flaps of Quickie Mouse and also through the cloth of your shirt. Quickie Mouse can sit right on your shoulder!

(33) STRIKE-IT-RICH MONEY WALLET

A dashing piece of gift wrap makes this easy-to-make wallet a fancy place to keep your allowance.

WHAT YOU'LL NEED

- gift wrap, 8 inches by 22 inches • strong craft glue • penny
- large paper clip, about 2 inches long

DIRECTIONS

1 Lay the printed side of the gift wrap face up on a flat surface with the longer edge toward you. Fold in half lengthwise and open flat. Fold the top right and top left edges flush with the center crease. Fold the bottom right and bottom left edges flush with the center crease.

2 Turn paper over. Fold the pointed-looking arrows on the right and left sides toward each other, not meeting in the middle but creasing at their bottom corners.

3 Fold paper lengthwise in half, folds tucked inside. Pull out the triangular corner inside the back flap on the right end. Tuck the triangle into the front flap on the right end. Pull out the triangular piece inside the front flap on the left end. Tuck the corner into the back flap on the left end. Fold the wallet in half widthwise.

4 Glue a penny to the end of a large paper clip opposite the end that clips paper together. Allow to dry.

5 Clip penny paper clip to the side of your wallet when you want to close it. Tuck a buck or two into this fancy money holder, and you are ready to hit the town!

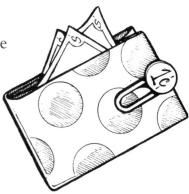

FANTASTIC FEATHER BOA

Adult Supervision Recommended

This costume-closet staple is a perfect addition for a cabaret singer's flounce prop.

WHAT YOU'LL NEED

● yarn ● scissors ● ruler ● yarn needle ● roll of colored toilet paper

DIRECTIONS

1 Cut a piece of yarn 5 feet long. Ask an adult to tie a knot in the yarn and thread an oversize yarn needle.

2 Pull a section of toilet paper about 2 feet long off the roll. Rumple into loose accordion pleats by starting at one end and gathering paper until you reach the other end.

3 Hold gathered strip in the middle and poke needle through the center of all the toilet-paper layers, stringing the bunch onto the yarn.

4 Repeat Steps 2 and 3 until tissue is strung over the entire length of yarn.

5 Remove the needle from the yarn. Tie the loose end of yarn into a thick knot and snip off any excess yarn end-pieces with scissors.

6 To give your boa a more feathered effect, make horizontal snips with the scissors at a 45-degree angle to both sides of the gathered paper's edges. Now twirl it, wear it around your neck, or attach it onto a Native American headdress . . . these flouncy "feathers" never shed!

EXTRA, EXTRA! FUNNY PAPER KITE

Adult Supervision Recommended

The Sunday comics from your local newspaper will give the birds in the sky something to laugh about!

WHAT YOU'LL NEED

- newspaper comics spread • scissors • eight self-adhesive mailing labels or name-tag labels, each at least 1½ inches by 3 inches • kite string
- needle with eye big enough to accommodate kite string

DIRECTIONS

1 Fold the bottom edge of a sheet of comics on the diagonal so it is flush with the top edge of the sheet. Use your scissors to trim off any leftover paper down the left side of the sheet. Now your comics sheet is a perfect square. Unfold.

2 Lay the square in a diamond shape, and fold down the top right edge to meet the center diagonal crease. Fold down the top left edge flush with the center diagonal crease.

3 Apply four labels, one atop the other, to the inside corner of one flap. Apply four more labels in the same fashion to the inside corner of the opposite flap. This will prevent your kite from tearing when you fly it.

4 Cut a piece of kite string several yards long (long enough to fly your kite) and thread the needle with this piece. Thread the needle through the paper and all the labels on the inner flaps. Tie these two pieces of string together about four or five inches away from the kite. Tie the end in a thick knot.

5 On a breezy day, run against the wind, letting the breeze lift your kite behind you. Don't forget to bring along a kite "first aid" kit: extra string, clear tape, and scissors.

ROYALTY MASKS

Adult Supervision Recommended

If the mark of royalty is a regal face, these clever disguises will make you a king or queen!

WHAT YOU'LL NEED

- paper plate • pencil • scissors • yellow construction paper • white glue
- markers in several colors • glitter glue in two or three different colors • yarn

DIRECTIONS

1 Hold the paper plate up to your face back-side out and have an adult lightly draw a general outline of your eyes, nose, and mouth with a pencil. Remove the plate from your face and cut out two tiny eye holes at the center of the pencil drawings. Hold the plate up to your face again. Can you see out of the holes? If you can't, make adjustments as necessary. Cut out both the nose and mouth outlines.

2 Cut yellow construction paper into the shape of a crown. With regular white glue, glue the crown to the very top of your mask and allow to dry. When dry, trim the sides so the crown is no wider than the plate.

3 Decorate the face of your mask with colored markers. Outline lips and make circles for cheeks and arches for eyebrows. Draw details on the crown, such as the outline of jewels. Then use glitter glue to outline the eye, nose, and mouth holes and to fill in the jewels of your crown. Allow to dry.

4 Cut two pieces of yarn, each about 1 foot long. Have an adult help you poke tiny holes on either side of the mask. Knot each piece of yarn on one end. Thread the yarn through the holes, with the knots showing on the front of the mask.

5 Try on your mask and tie the yarn in a bow behind your head. When friends address you, make sure they first say, "Your Highness"!

WINTER WIZARD HAT

Adult Supervision Recommended

Glittery snowflakes decorate the headdress of a mythical Winter Wizard. Wear this costume piece when winter weather rules—or anytime of year you want to put a crisp, wintery magic in the air!

WHAT YOU'LL NEED

- 3 yards of tissue streamer • scissors • 22-inch square of poster board
- ruler • glue • paper clips • silver and gold gift wrap • pencil

DIRECTIONS

1 Cut streamer into three pieces, each a yard long. Place poster board square in a diamond shape, corner pointing toward you. Place one end of a streamer about 6 inches below the top corner of the poster board (the rest of the streamer juts out above the top corner of the poster board). Glue down a small section of the streamer to the poster board. Align another streamer on top of the first streamer and glue it to the first streamer. Glue the last streamer onto the second streamer in the same fashion. Allow glue to dry.

2 Bring the right and left corners of the poster board toward the center of the diamond, forming a cone shape (streamers jut out of the top of the cone). Overlap the right and left corners at least 3 inches. Holding the corners together, place the hat on your head to see how it fits. Tighten or loosen as needed, then glue the seam together. Attach paper clips to the overlapping section to hold the cone shape while the glue dries.

3 Cut gold and silver gift wrap into 4-inch squares—about four squares of each color will do. Fold one square in half diagonally.

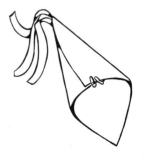

4 Fold triangle in half lengthwise. Fold triangle in half again. Use scissors to snip out shapes from all sides of the triangle. Try cutting out rounded half circles or long triangular shapes. Unfold, and you have a delicate snowflake! Repeat this process with all your squares.

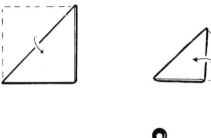 

5 Glue silver and gold snowflakes in random spots all over the outside of the cone hat. Allow glue to dry before putting the cone hat on your head. Have an adult draw a pencil line around the bottom of the cone showing where the cone should be cut to even out the bottom edge. Remove cone hat and cut along that line. Now your hat is ready to wear.

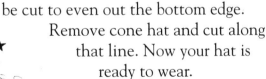

NATURE'S TREASURE BOX

An environmentally friendly box is ideal for storing odd-looking stones and other weird treasures from Mother Nature.

WHAT YOU'LL NEED

- four sheets of tissue, each in a different shade of a family of colors (such as dark purple, dark blue, royal blue, and violet) • scissors
- empty cardboard egg carton • glue • twenty-four cotton balls • pen
- 3-by-5-inch index card • clear tape

DIRECTIONS

1 Stack the four sheets of tissue paper on top of one another. Cut paper into various shapes. Triangles, squares, rectangles, squiggles, and circles are all good choices. Make sure to cut through all layers of tissue.

2 Take the egg carton and glue a single tissue shape to its lid. Glue more tissue shapes to the lid in the same fashion. Shapes can overlap or lay side by side in any pattern you like. Every edge of tissue should be secured to the carton. Cover the entire carton, then open it and cover the inside of the carton's lid, too. The holes in the front of the carton help secure it closed. Do not cover these!

3 Fluff out each cotton ball by pulling it gently in opposite directions. Glue two cotton balls in each egg compartment of the carton. Set aside to dry.

4 Now take a trip outdoors. Look for an interesting pebble, a tiny leaf, a small flower, or any other object found in nature that is small enough to fit in a compartment of your nature box. Place your find on top of the cotton balls. Then see if you can identify the item's specific name. You can use a reference book, or ask an adult for help. List your treasure on a 3-by-5-inch index card and tape the card in the lid of your box so you know just what's in your collection!

39 SWIRLS OF COLOR COASTER

Put old magazine pages to work by making a hip-looking coaster that protects tabletops from both hot and cold drinks.

WHAT YOU'LL NEED

- magazine that you can tear pages from • six drinking straws (long, skinny paper straws work best) • clear tape • glue

DIRECTIONS

1 Tear a colorful page out of a magazine. On a flat surface, lay a straw across the lower right-hand corner of the magazine page. Holding the corner of the page to the straw, begin rolling the straw diagonally across the page. Roll the magazine page tightly around the straw on the diagonal until the page is completely wrapped around the straw. Secure the magazine page around the straw by wrapping a piece of clear tape around the middle of the long tube and two more pieces of tape around the tube an inch from each end.

2 Begin coiling the tube into a flat circle by rolling in one end, wrapping the tube around itself until the other end is reached. Use clear tape to secure the end of the tube to the coil.

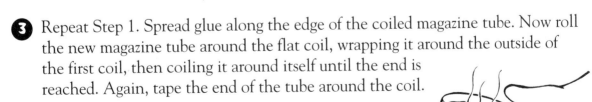

3 Repeat Step 1. Spread glue along the edge of the coiled magazine tube. Now roll the new magazine tube around the flat coil, wrapping it around the outside of the first coil, then coiling it around itself until the end is reached. Again, tape the end of the tube around the coil.

4 Repeat Step 3 with the four remaining straws and magazine pages. Allow glue to dry and your coaster is ready to use.

JAMMIN' TAMBOURINE

Rock out with this streamer tambourine! It's a radical rhythm-maker that looks cool when you shake and twirl it in a circle.

WHAT YOU'LL NEED

- 6 yards of inch-wide cloth ribbon • ruler • scissors • two paper plates
- ⅓ cup dry lentils or beans • five pennies • glue • colored pens

DIRECTIONS

1 Measure and cut ribbon into nine pieces, each 2 feet long.

2 Set a paper plate right side up on a flat surface. Spacing them equally, arrange all nine ribbons so they jut out from the inside of the paper plate like rays from the sun. The end of each ribbon should be 2 or 3 inches in from the rim of the plate. Glue each ribbon to the inside of the paper plate. Allow glue to dry.

3 Place ⅓ cup of dry lentils or beans and five pennies in the middle of the paper plate with the glued ribbons. Apply a line of glue all along the rim of the plate. Place the second paper plate face-down atop the first, gluing them together. Set aside to dry.

4 When your tambourine has dried, use colored pens to decorate both sides with stars and musical notes. In big letters, write your name or the name of your band across one side of the tambourine. Now jam out to your favorite tunes!

SANDPAPER IMPRESSIONS

Adult Supervision Required

You become an Impressionist when you make these beautiful—yet simple—prints. Their dotty texture makes them look so sophisticated you'll want to show them off, so plan on making one or two extra prints for your friends.

WHAT YOU'LL NEED

- crayons in bold, bright colors • medium-rough sandpaper (no bigger than your construction paper) • paper towels • ironing board • newspaper • white construction paper • iron

DIRECTIONS

1 Color a striking design with your crayons on the rough side of a piece of sandpaper. Some cool subjects for your crayon drawing are an instrument you'd like to play, an exotic landscape, or a mythical creature. The less detail in your drawing, the better it will transfer. Try to get as much crayon into the grain of the sandpaper as you can. If you write any word, be sure to write it backward so it will read correctly when you iron it.

2 Lay paper towels over the ironing board (so it doesn't get dirty from the newsprint), then lay several sheets of newspaper over the paper towels. Place the sandpaper drawing on the newspaper, rough side up. Place one piece of white construction paper directly over the sandpaper.

3 Have an adult help you iron over the top of the construction paper at the iron's lowest setting until the crayon melts. Remove the construction paper and set aside to cool. Now that's *impressive!*

51

42 LOOK-WHO'S-BOSS BADGE

This badge may have a funny face, but it spells out who's in charge.
Wear this triangle pin when it's your turn to lead.

WHAT YOU'LL NEED

- white construction paper • cardboard • pencil • ruler • scissors
- metal paper fastener • safety pin • clear tape • glue • 6 inches of yarn
- colored markers

DIRECTIONS

1 On a piece of cardboard, draw a triangle 3 inches in dimension on every side with your pencil. Cut it out. Trace the cardboard cutout on a sheet of white construction paper, and with a ruler, add about ¾ inch all around. Cut the triangle out of the construction paper.

2 Open the metal fastener slightly and slide one side of the fastener through the closed side of a safety pin. Use scissors to make a hole in the center of the cardboard triangle. Push the fastener through the hole in the triangle and open it flush with the cardboard. Place a piece of tape over the opened fastener. The safety pin should be able to open and close.

3 Glue the construction-paper triangle to the cardboard triangle on the same side the tape is attached. Fold the construction-paper triangle's edges around the cardboard triangle and glue them down.

4 Cut 6 inches of yarn into three pieces. Glue the short strands of yarn sticking up from the back side of the triangle's top corner, making hair for the boss. With colored markers, add two eyes, a nose, and a smiling mouth. At the bottom of the badge, use markers to spell out B-O-S-S.

5 To wear your badge, attach the safety pin to your shirt. Now look who's boss!

HAWAIIAN HULA SKIRT

You'll feel like dancing when you wear the traditional Hawaiian festive attire. Create your own dancing duds and hula the day away!

WHAT YOU'LL NEED

- newspaper ● green poster paint ● paintbrush about 3 inches wide
- 2 yards of 1-inch-wide ribbon ● scissors ● glue

DIRECTIONS

1 Lay out newspaper to protect your work area. Unfold two large sheets of newspaper and place them side by side on your work area. Use a wide paintbrush to paint both sheets green. Allow the paint to dry, then turn both sheets over and paint the other side. Allow paint to dry.

2 Slide the edge of one green sheet over on top of the edge of the other, creating an overlap of approximately 3 inches. Place the ribbon in a horizontal line about 3 inches below the top edge of the newspapers. The ribbon should hang out only about 7 inches on either side of the newspapers. Trim off any excess.

3 Fold the top edge of the newspapers over the ribbon. Glue the edges of the fold down, allowing the ribbon to slide back and forth inside the loop of paper. Allow glue to dry.

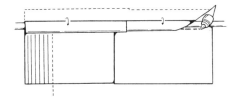

4 Make vertical cuts in the newspapers from the bottom edge, stopping just before the glued waistband. The strips should be no more than 1 inch wide.

5 To wear the grass skirt, hold the waistband at one end of the skirt against your waist and wrap the other end of the skirt around as many times as it will go. Then tie the two ends of the ribbons together. Now you are ready to dance!

PURPLE PAL FROM THE DEEP

Give your friends a good laugh when you display your own octopus as a tabletop centerpiece. And its arms hold things, too!

WHAT YOU'LL NEED

- newspaper • scissors • ruler • plastic spoon • measuring cups • glue
- water • mixing bowl • round gallon-sized ice-cream container
- poster paint • paintbrushes

DIRECTIONS

1 Cover work area with newspaper. Cut a separate sheet of newspaper into about thirty strips, each 2 inches wide and 20 inches long. With a plastic spoon, mix approximately 1 cup of white glue and ⅔ cup water together in a bowl.

2 Set the container upside down on the newspaper. Dip one newspaper strip into the glue mixture. Hold the strip by one end over the bowl and quickly run two fingers down both sides of the entire strip, working off the excess glue. Drape the middle of the strip over the container and let both ends fall on either side of the container—these are the octopus's legs. Repeat with another strip crossing the first one in the middle. Add two more strips at a diagonal to the others. Now your octopus has eight legs.

3 In the same order, layer the next four strips exactly over the existing ones, then add one more layer to the legs with four more strips of newspaper. Curl the ends of the legs up, as if they are holding a cup. Take the remaining strips and wrap them clockwise around the container. Keep wrapping strips around the octopus body until the outside of the container is completely covered. Wash out your mixing bowl and throw away the plastic spoon. Allow your octopus to dry overnight.

4 When the octopus is dry, its legs may have attached to the newsprint you were working on. Simply tear away any excess paper. Use purple poster paint to give it coloring and other colors of paint for a kooky face! First paint the top and sides of the creature. Allow paint to dry, then paint the octopus's underside. Turn the animal upside down to dry. When the legs have dried, paint on bright blue suckers on the underside of the octopus's legs.

ONE STEP FURTHER

Decorate a food table at your next party with this goofy sea creature. Stick a bottle of ketchup in one arm, some mustard in another, and plenty of napkins in the other arms.

PAPER PETALS BOUQUET

Flowers that last forever are perfect room decorations. Or, give these blooms away and collect smiles in return!

WHAT YOU'LL NEED

- various colors of tissue paper • ruler • scissors • clear tape • pipe cleaners

DIRECTIONS

1 To make a mum, cut three 6-inch squares of tissue paper. Take one square and fold it in half diagonally. Then fold it in half diagonally two more times. Hold the corner (the one with all folded edges) of the tissue triangle. Cut an outward curve from one remaining corner to the other.

2 Repeat with the other two tissue squares, making each one shorter than the last by starting the curve closer to the point you are holding. Open all tissues and stack them atop one another, the largest on the bottom and the smallest on top.

3 Poke one finger into the center of all the tissues and use your other hand to gather the tissues up around that finger. Twist the bottom of the tissues in one direction, forming a short stem. Secure the twist by wrapping it in clear tape. Fluff the petals out for a mum in full bloom!

4 Attach stem to a pipe cleaner by twisting the two together to create an even longer stem. Now make a whole bouquet of mums in different colors!

ONE STEP FURTHER

Spritz a bit of your favorite perfume on the petals to give your flowers an awesome scent.

PAPER MAGIC

Surprise your friends by magically turning a tiny rectangle into a big circle with a snippity snip!

WHAT YOU'LL NEED

- business card • scissors

DIRECTIONS

1 Fold business card in half lengthwise. Make a vertical cut ¼ inch from the top left side. Cut should start at the folded edge and should stop short ¼ inch from the other side. Make a similar vertical cut ¼ inch from the top right side. Now cut horizontally along the fold between the two end cuts.

2 Make another vertical cut ¼ inch from the end cut on the right, but this time the cut comes from the opposite direction, stopping ¼ inch from the *folded* edge. Alternate cutting sides to form pattern shown in illustration.

3 Carefully unfold the card, and you'll have a circle big enough to stand in!

4 When you've practiced the trick, gather friends around and say, "Before your eyes I will turn this tiny rectangular business card into a circle large enough for one person to step inside." When you perform your trick, your friends will be amazed you were telling the truth!

DANCING STICK MAN

Adult Supervision Recommended

Become a puppeteer with the ultra-flexible Stick Man puppet. He's easy to manipulate and loves to rock to your favorite tunes.

WHAT YOU'LL NEED

- two pencils (one unsharpened) ● drinking glass ● heavy, white paper
- ruler ● colored markers ● scissors ● seven metal paper fasteners
- strong craft glue

DIRECTIONS

1 First draw a figure eight. To do this, use a pencil to trace the bottom of a glass onto white paper, making a perfect circle. Then trace another circle directly above the first.

2 On another section of the paper, draw four oblong shapes (these are for the upper and lower portions of the legs). The shapes should be about 3 inches tall and 1 inch wide. Draw a foot at the bottom end of two of the shapes.

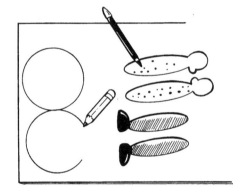

3 Draw two arms, each about ¾ inch wide and 3½ inches long. Draw a hand at the end of each arm.

4 Use colored markers to draw a happy face for Stick Man in the top circle of the figure eight. Make the lower portion of the figure eight his body. Give him fun clothing; for instance, his shirt and pants could have a wild polka-dot or plaid pattern.

5 Cut out each shape from the paper. Lay Stick Man out on a flat surface, arranging his body parts in their approximate location. With a pencil, mark a dot on the back of each shape near the end where it should connect with the next piece. Have an adult use the point of your scissors to pierce the dot or dots on each piece.

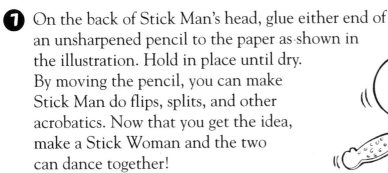

6 Match the holes of each piece to its connecting limb by overlapping the two. When the holes are lined up, push a brad through both holes. Open the brad on the back side of the paper.

7 On the back of Stick Man's head, glue either end of an unsharpened pencil to the paper as shown in the illustration. Hold in place until dry. By moving the pencil, you can make Stick Man do flips, splits, and other acrobatics. Now that you get the idea, make a Stick Woman and the two can dance together!

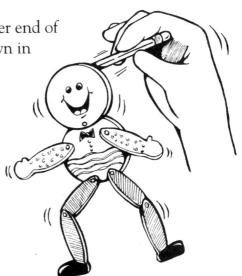

HEAD FOR HATS

Two heads are better than one, especially when the extra head is helping you keep track of your hats!

WHAT YOU'LL NEED

- newspaper • scissors • ruler • 2 cups glue • 1½ cups water
- mixing bowl • spoon • balloon • needle or straight pin
- paintbrushes • poster paint in different colors

DIRECTIONS

1 Cover your work area with newspaper. Cut additional newspaper into strips of various lengths, about 1½ inches wide. Mix the glue and water in a big bowl with a spoon.

2 Blow up a round balloon and tie the end. Dip newspaper strips into the glue mixture. Remove excess glue by holding one end of each strip over the bowl and quickly running two fingers down both sides of the strip to the other end.

3 Drape strips over the top of the balloon. Also wind strips horizontally around the balloon. Keep applying strips to the balloon until it is completely covered in at least two layers of paper strips. Do not wrap strips around the bottom of the balloon, however, because you don't want a complete ball shape that will roll. Instead, let the lower strips fall over the newspaper covering your work area, creating a shape more like a head sitting on shoulders.

4 Place more strips around the bottom of the balloon where it meets your work area, giving it a stable base so it will stand on its own.

5 Clean your mixing bowl, spoon, and work area. Allow head to dry overnight.

6 When the head is completely dry, poke a needle or straight pin into the papier-mâché, popping the balloon. Some of the base strips will be sticking to the newspaper layer you covered your work area with. Just trim off any extra paper not needed to hold up the head.

7 Use poster paint to give a base coat to your head, painting it entirely with one neutral color. Allow the base coat to dry. Next paint the entire face one color and paint the hair another color. Allow to dry. Lastly, paint in the features of the friendly face on your head and add any details to the hair, such as curls in a different shade or barrettes. Make sure every bit of papier-mâché is covered with your creative painting. Set aside to dry. This bright head wears your hat when you do not. Now you can't lose your hat without losing your head, too!

SOX BOX

Surprise the folks by being ultra-organized with this designer sock drawer. It keeps sets of socks together so you're never without a pair!

WHAT YOU'LL NEED

- ruler • shallow or cut-off cardboard box (no taller than 4 inches)
- pencil • poster board • scissors • newspaper • poster paint
- paintbrush, at least 2 inches wide

DIRECTIONS

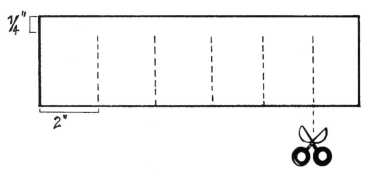

1 Measure the height and length of your cardboard box. With a pencil, draw a rectangle the same height and length of your box on a piece of poster board. Draw a second rectangle the exact same size as the one you just drew. Cut out both from the poster board. These will be insets in your Sox Box.

2 Measure 2 inches in from the two short ends of one rectangle, and with your pencil mark a straight vertical line down each side. From the top edge, cut along one vertical line, stopping ¼ inch before the bottom edge. Cut the opposite vertical line in the same fashion. Make three more identical cuts equally spaced from one another between the end cuts. Each cut should stop ¼ inch from the bottom edge. Repeat with second rectangle.

3 Measure the height and width of your cardboard box. Draw a rectangle the same height and width on the poster board. Draw two more rectangles the exact same size. Cut all three out of the poster board.

4 Place the first two long insets across the length of your box, then insert the three dividers through the cuts in the poster board. Your box is now divided into twelve sections.

5 Line your work area with newspaper. Use poster paint to give your box a one-color finish. Allow to dry, then paint one more coat. Allow that coat to dry as well. You may want to personalize your box by writing your name in large letters or adding stickers.

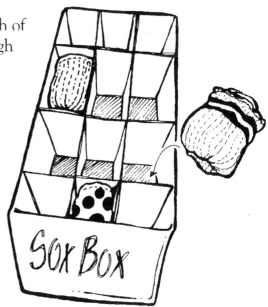

6 Roll socks into pairs and store one pair in each cubical. With each pair in its place, you'll never go unmatched!

Adult Supervision Recommended

You can help the environment by recycling paper to create your own! Your homemade paper's beautiful, natural texture makes it an ideal canvas for a nature poem or picture.

WHAT YOU'LL NEED

- wax paper • blender • water • 2 tablespoons glue
- two full sheets of newspaper torn to shreds • toilet tissue
- rolling pin • sponge • fine-point felt-tipped pen

DIRECTIONS

1 Line the flat surface you'll be working on with wax paper. Fill blender half full of water. Add glue and a heaping handful of shredded newspaper. With an adult's help, blend paper into the water. Gradually add toilet tissue until you have a thick, wet pulp mixture.

2 Pour pulp mixture onto wax paper. Flatten with your hands. Roll a rolling pin over the mixture, forming a thin, smooth piece of paper. Blot the excess water that rolls onto the wax paper with a sponge. Let paper dry overnight.

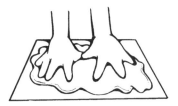 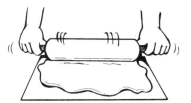

3 When paper is dry, it's time to use your imagination. Do you like to hike, climb a tree, or watch birds? Using your pen on the recycled paper, write a poem or draw a picture about different ways to help save the environment.